Thank you to Jean L.,
an author with manners.

For Noé, Basile, Anaé, and Élio,
children with manners… almost.

— M. M.

A Well-Mannered Young Wolf

Written by
Jean Leroy

Illustrated by
Matthieu Maudet

GROWL

EERDMANS BOOKS FOR YOUNG READERS

GRAND RAPIDS, MICHIGAN

A young wolf, whose parents had taught him good manners,

went hunting alone in the forest for the first time.

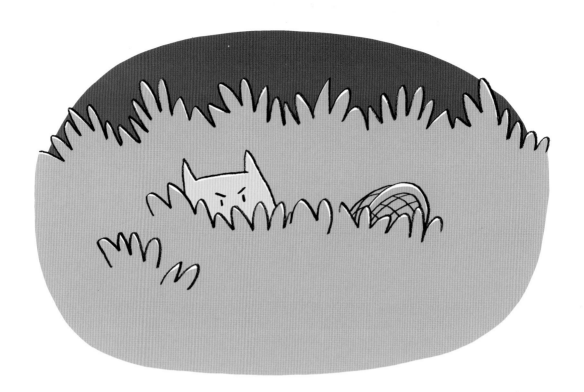

Very quickly, he caught . . .

a rabbit!

The young wolf, of course, did not have a book with him. But his parents had taught him that a last wish must always be respected.

When the young wolf returned with his favorite book under his arm, the rabbit had vanished.

Wait . . . he's gone?

Oh, that liar!

The young hunter stormed off
in search of other prey.

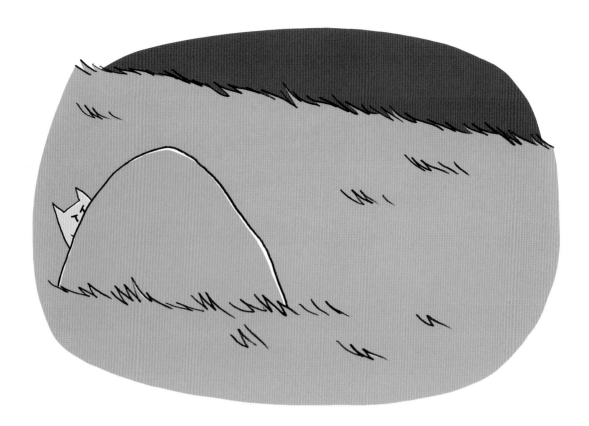

And he captured . . .

a chicken!

What is your last wish?
Uh . . . freedom?
Impossible. I'm too hungry!
Then I'd like you to play me some music!
I have a good book. Wouldn't you prefer a story?
No, no! I want music! Remember, a last wish . . .
. . . must always be respected. I know!

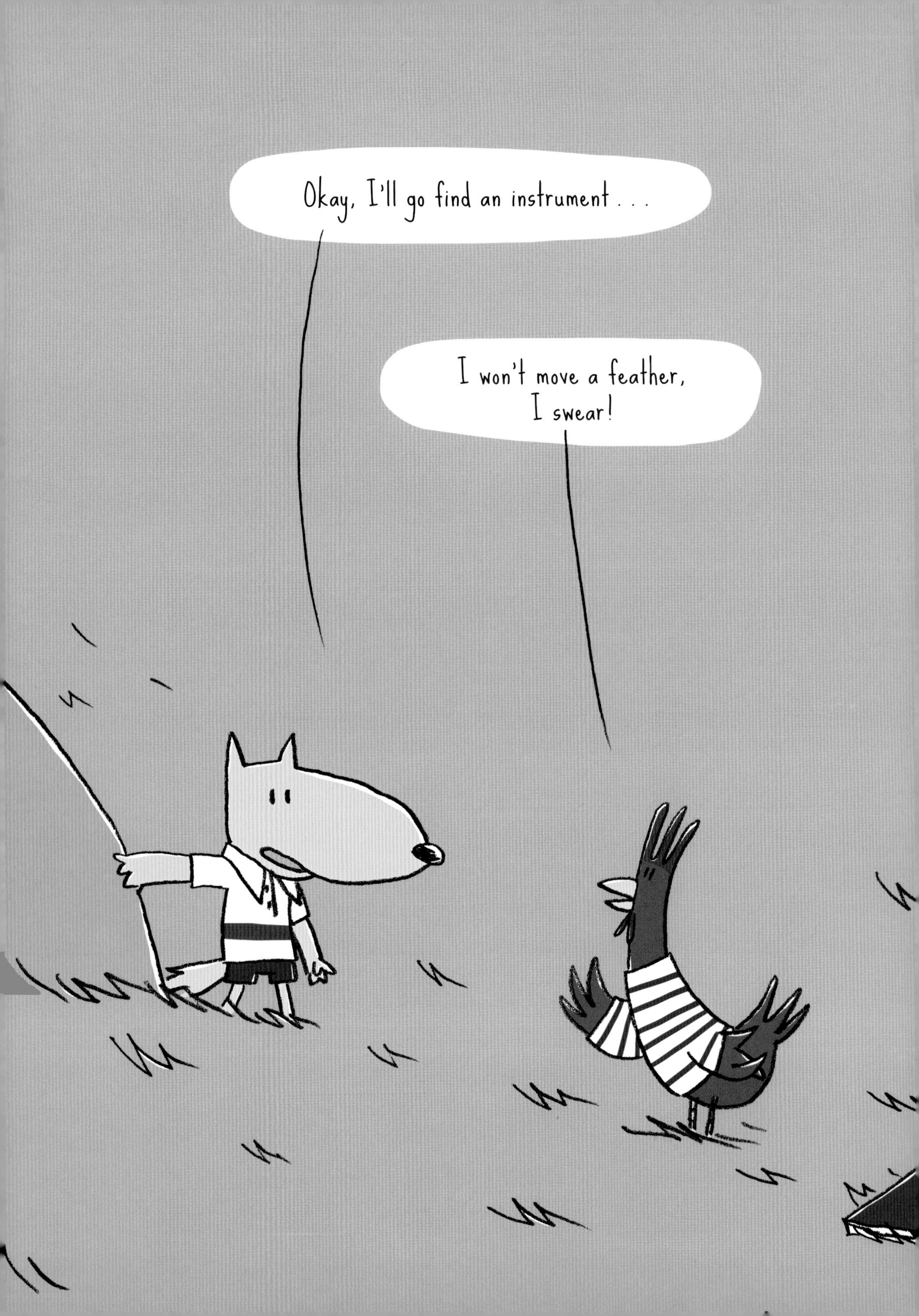
Okay, I'll go find an instrument . . .
I won't move a feather, I swear!

But the chicken didn't wait for the wolf either.

Furious, the hunter resumed his search
for more prey to devour.

Soon he found . . .

a little boy!

At the idea of having to return home a third time,
the young hunter exploded with rage.

But the little boy hadn't asked for his freedom. And he'd also said please. The wolf groaned and went back to his house.

It's magnificent!
Thank you very much!

And now . . .

Okay, fine.
But be quick. I'm hungry!

You're going to eat me already?
What a shame! I'd like to show my
drawing to my friends.

Jean Leroy worked as a teacher for ten years before becoming a full-time writer. He has written dozens of children's books, several of which have been published in multiple languages. He lives in France. Visit his website at www.jeanleroy.wordpress.com.

Matthieu Maudet studied graphic design in France and now devotes himself completely to illustrating children's books. He started collaborating with Jean Leroy in 2005; since then, they have published over a dozen picture books together. Visit his website at www.matthieumaudet.blogspot.com.

First published in the United States in 2016 by
Eerdmans Books for Young Readers,
an imprint of Wm. B. Eerdmans Publishing Co.
2140 Oak Industrial Dr. NE
Grand Rapids, Michigan 49505

www.eerdmans.com/youngreaders

Originally published in France in 2013 under the title
Un jeune loup bien éduqué
by l'école des loisirs, Paris, France

Text by Jean Leroy
Illustrations by Matthieu Maudet
© 2013 l'école des loisirs
This English edition © Eerdmans Books for Young Readers

Manufactured at Tien Wah Press in Malaysia

22 21 20 19 18 17 16   9 8 7 6 5 4 3 2 1

ISBN 978-0-8028-5479-7

A catalog listing is available from the Library of Congress.

The display type was set in Gil Sans.
The text type was set in Gil Sans.
The dialogue type was set in Sue Ellen Francisco.